SKYE
The Champion

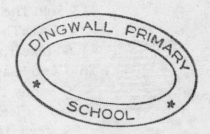

DINGWALL PRIMARY
SCHOOL

Home Farm Twins

Skye

The Champion

Jenny Oldfield

Illustrated by Kate Aldous

*Hodder
Children's
Books*

a division of Hodder Headline plc

Copyright © 1998 Jenny Oldfield
Illustrations copyright © 1998 Kate Aldous

First published in Great Britain in 1998
by Hodder Children's Books

The right of Jenny Oldfield to be identified as the Author of
the Work has been asserted by her in accordance with the
Copyright, Designs and Patents Act 1988.

10 9 8 7 6 5 4 3 2 1

All rights reserved. No part of this publication may be
reproduced, stored in a retrieval system, or transmitted,
in any form or by any means without the prior written
permission of the publisher, nor be otherwise circulated
in any form of binding or cover other than that in which
it is published and without a similar condition being
imposed on the subsequent purchaser.

All characters in this publication are fictitious
and any resemblance to real persons, living or dead,
is purely coincidental.

A Catalogue record for this book is available from the British Library

ISBN 0 340 69985 X

Typeset by Avon Dataset Ltd, Bidford-on-Avon, Warks

Printed and bound in Great Britain by
Mackays of Chatham plc, Chatham, Kent

Hodder Children's Books
a division of Hodder Headline plc
338 Euston Road
London NW1 3BH

One

'Swee-eet!' Hannah Moore climbed the ramp into Fred Hunt's trailer. Two young Friesian calves stared back at her with their big, dark eyes.

Hannah's twin sister, Helen, handed her bundles of straw to make bedding for the young cows. 'They're gorgeous!' she agreed.

The gangly black-and-white calves poked their broad pink noses at Hannah, nuzzling up to her as she worked. They looked as if butter wouldn't melt in their mouths.

Nuzzle-nuzzle with their noses. Then, *whack*! One of the calves butted her with its hard head.

'Hey!' Hannah overbalanced and fell against the side of the metal trailer. The calf licked her face with its rough tongue, while the other lurched down the ramp in a sudden bid for freedom.

'Never mind "sweet" and "gorgeous"!' Mr Hunt grumbled as he grabbed the fleeing calf by the halter rope. He poked his head inside the trailer. 'I've just paid good money for these two weanlings, so you watch what you're doing!'

'B-but . . . !' Hannah protested. She had straw in her hair and was in danger of being licked to death by the second eager calf. Outside the trailer, the bustle of the cattle auction continued.

'It wasn't Hannah's fault,' Helen explained. Over the grumpy old farmer's shoulder she could see her dad grinning at the mess Hannah was in.

Fred Hunt tutted. He held tight to the eight-week-old stock calf which he'd just bought. 'Never blame the beast if anything goes wrong,' he insisted. 'Blame the stockman!'

He handed the rope to Helen, then went and hauled Hannah to her feet with a strong arm. He pulled her down the ramp and out of the way.

David Moore came forward and nodded. 'Good

advice, girls. It's the same as saying "a bad workman blames his tools". You should listen to what Fred says.'

Silently Hannah rubbed her elbows and her knees, while her dad picked straw out of her dark hair. The last thing they wanted now was a lecture.

They got one anyway as their unflappable, dogged neighbour from High Hartwell Farm went on.

'For instance, if you want to lead a calf up a ramp, don't pull on the rope,' he warned Helen. 'Just put two fingers inside her mouth and let her suck.'

Helen stared. 'Inside her mouth?' she echoed.

'Go on, what are you waiting for?' A smile played about the corners of Fred Hunt's lips. 'It won't hurt!'

So she did as she was told. She felt the strong, soft, warm suck of the young calf.

'That's it. Now she'll follow you anywhere you like!'

It was true. Helen walked into the trailer with the calf clinging like a limpet to her fingers. The trailer had metal sides and an arched metal roof, and there was just room inside for the two animals Fred had bought. Soon both calves were tethered fast and the ramp was lifted.

'Are you pleased with them?' David Moore asked
the farmer, once the new stock was safe and sound.

Fred grunted and lifted his cap to scratch his head.
'Nice, glossy coats, a clear eye and a clean nose and
mouth.' He leaned over the tail-board and cast an
expert eye over the Friesians. 'They're alert beasts,
neither cringing nor bullying . . .'

'Huh!' Hannah was still dusting herself down. She,
Helen and their dad had come to the autumn market
in Nesfield as a half-term treat. It was their first visit
to the maze of pens and show-rings since they'd
come to live at Home Farm.

'Don't bring any sweet little calves back with you!' their mum, Mary Moore, had warned. 'Because sweet little calves have a habit of growing up into hulking great cows, and we already have our hands *quite* full enough, thank you!'

She knew the twins were likely to fall in love with anything that had four legs. So they'd promised to look but not buy. They'd arrived at Nesfield market in time to see their neighbour snap up two of the best stock calves in the auction.

'As I was saying, they're nice enough beasts,' Fred Hunt went on now. 'But it'll cost me the earth to keep them going over the winter.' He bolted the door and shuffled round to the Land-rover, which was going to tow the trailer back over the fells to his dairy farm.

'I thought cows only ate grass.' Helen couldn't see why he was grumbling.

The farmer huffed and puffed his way into the driving seat. 'Only grass! "From Christmas to May, cattle fall away." Haven't you heard that saying?'

She shook her head.

'Winter's coming. They'll need hay and calf nuts to get them through. Then I'll have to build extra calf pens to house them out of the cold. I'll have to get them vaccinated against pneumonia, diarrhoea and scours.' Fred Hunt glumly listed all the expenses of dairy farming. 'They'll need to be dosed for worms and tested for tuberculosis, brucellosis . . .'

'Stop, stop!' David Moore held up his hands in mock horror.

Helen and Hannah heard the torrent of long words with real dismay. It seemed there were a dozen terrible things that could go wrong with the calves.

'Don't worry,' their dad murmured as Fred Hunt's Land-rover chugged across the stockyard to join the queue at the gate. The heads of his calves were just visible over the tail-board of the trailer. 'Fred likes to grumble, but really he's very pleased.'

'Pleased?' Hannah looked wide-eyed at her dad.

David Moore nodded. 'He just has a funny way of showing it, that's all.' He smiled at the girls. 'Come on, let's follow him back to Doveton and help him unload.'

So they jumped into their own car and joined the slow-moving queue, weaving between the groups of sturdy, Lakeland farmers and their cattle.

On the back seat, Hannah rubbed her bruised

elbows, craning for a view of Mr Hunt and his two new calves. 'Swee-eet!' she murmured again. In spite of everything, she couldn't resist their white faces and big, dark eyes.

'Make way there, make way!' A man leaned out of his car window and yelled at the other drivers in the queue out of the market yard. 'I'm in a hurry to get out!'

'Fat chance!' David Moore murmured, glancing in his overhead mirror at the traffic jam.

Helen turned to look. The car was big and silver. It gleamed in the autumn sun. The man who was shouting didn't look like a farmer in his brown suede jacket and dark green polo shirt.

'Let me through!' He pressed his car horn, making some nearby cattle skitter sideways.

'Who's that?' Hannah wanted to know. The silver car came alongside, blaring its horn and jumping the queue.

'Terence Cooke,' their dad told them through gritted teeth. '*Lord* Terence Cooke of Coningsby Hall!'

'Is he really a lord?' Hannah gasped. She caught

sight of a frowning, tanned face and slicked back grey hair.

'No, but he acts like one.' David Moore gave way to the car as it nudged its long, shiny bonnet forward through the crowd. 'What does he think he's playing at?'

They watched the man nose to the front of the queue, where Fred Hunt's Land-rover and trailer sat waiting to turn on to the main road.

'Get a move on, why don't you!' Cooke yelled.

Instead, Fred Hunt put on his handbrake and opened his door. He stepped out of his cab.

'Uh-oh,' Helen muttered. All eyes were on the stubborn old farmer as he walked towards Terence Cooke's silver car and leaned an arm along its roof. He tilted his cap back and peered in at the driver.

'What's your hurry?' Fred asked in a loud voice.

'Come on, man, get your trailer out of my way!' Mr Cooke yelled back.

'Bad move!' Hannah tut-tutted. Even she could see that.

Fred stood his ground. 'I've got stock in that trailer,' he warned. 'I move when I like, as fast or as slow as I like. Anyway, what's your hurry?'

Cooke glared up at him. 'If you must know, my stockman got held up with two beasts he's bringing to market. He's late, and I want to know why!'

'Is Mr Cooke a farmer?' Helen heard the word, stockman, and was taken aback. Terence Cooke didn't look anything like the tweedy, woolly, weather-beaten farmers round here.

'Is Coningsby Hall a farm, then?' Hannah echoed the surprise.

'Sort of.' David Moore kept an eye on the developing row and told Hannah and Helen all he knew. 'I've heard the old timers like Fred talking about him. Apparently he breeds rare animals up there as a kind of hobby. Highland cattle and suchlike.'

'Are they the ones with shaggy coats?' Helen asked, taking a sudden, lively interest.

'And big, curly horns?' Hannah added.

'They're the ones.' Their dad watched Fred Hunt shake his head at the furious landowner. 'He keeps a small herd of them, along with a few Kerrys and Dexters. He's interested in anything unusual. But I've heard Fred say to John Fox that he "reckons nowt" to Cooke and his fancy cattle. There's no love lost between them, as you can see!'

'But he can't be *all* bad,' Helen objected.

'Not if he likes animals,' Hannah agreed.

'Tell that to Fred Hunt!' David Moore saw the way the row was going; the old farmer trudging back to his Land-rover at a deliberate snail's pace, Cooke pressing hard on his horn, the Land-rover inching forward at last.

The twins' father sighed with relief as the queue started to move again. 'It could've been worse, I suppose.'

Tempers had frayed and snapped, but there had been no fight. Now Mr Cooke slid out through the gate and sped off along the road into town to see his stockman. He overtook Fred's trailer on a bend, then braked, before they lost sight of him altogether. Soon the Moores' own car was tailing Fred Hunt's and there was peace on the road once more.

' "*Whose pigs are these*?" ' David Moore sang at the top of his voice, as they passed a field of fat black and pink Old Spots. His good nature soon let him forget the row at the market.

' "*Whose pigs are these*?" ' Helen and Hannah shouted in chorus.

' "*They are John Potts*' "',' Hannah crowed.

' "*I can tell 'em by the spots,*" ' Helen added.

' "*And I found 'em in the vicarage ga-arden*!" '
All three finished the song together.

The pig field whizzed by, the road sign telling
them they were entering Nesfield as old-fashioned
grey stone houses began to line the sides of the
road.

'Look, there's Mr Cooke!' Hannah glimpsed the
big silver car ahead, in front of Fred Hunt's trailer.

'He's had to stop at traffic lights,' Helen pointed
out. 'What was the point of speeding off like that?'

The lights changed to green. Cooke signalled
right, and took off up the hill. Fred kept straight
ahead. David Moore pulled after him, just as the
lights began to change back to red.

Then there was a blur; a brown Land-rover driving
down the hill, jumping the lights, heading straight
for the side of the car. Hannah turned her head at
the last second. 'Dad, stop!' she screamed.

He jammed on the brakes. The Land-rover was
towing a brand new trailer. It kept on coming.

Helen braced herself against the seat in front. She
felt the force of the emergency brakes throw her

forward, heard the crunch of metal as the big four wheel drive hurtled into them. She slammed sideways against the door, felt Hannah land against her and looked up as the trailer behind the Land-rover swung round and jack-knifed into the air.

Two

After the noise of the crash came silence.

To Hannah and Helen it seemed to go on for a long time. Then their dad's voice was saying over and over, 'Are you both OK?' And then everything went frantic again.

Car doors slammed, footsteps ran, voices shouted.

'Helen, Hannah, are you hurt?' David Moore released his seat-belt and turned to look.

'No!' Helen whispered. She stared at the brown Land-rover that had ploughed into them, saw that the trailer had broken loose. It had tilted, slid across the road and tipped into the nearby ditch. 'I'm fine!'

'How about you, Hannah?' His anxious face peered into the back of the car.

'I'm OK.' She pulled herself upright with the sound of bellowing ringing through her head. It came from the upturned trailer; a frightened creature in pain. 'What happened?'

'Let's find out.' Their father's face was grim as he realised that his door was jammed. He climbed over the passenger seat and stepped out on to the road. The crashed cars blocked the crossroads, other drivers had stopped to stare.

Hannah put her hands over her ears to drown the terrified cries of the trapped animal. She followed Helen out of their car and round the back of the damaged Land-rover to where the trailer lay in the ditch.

'Steady!' A familiar voice broke through. It was Fred Hunt striding back along the road to the scene. He must have seen the accident in his mirror, pulled in and come to the rescue. 'Let's see what's what, shall we?' He pushed his way through the small knot of onlookers, ready to help.

The Land-rover driver stood by his vehicle, pale and shocked. But he raised his head at the sound of

Fred's voice, looking round anxiously at the spot where the trailer had ended up.

'What have you got in there, Edward?' Fred snapped, recognising the driver at once. 'How many beasts?'

'Two. A cow and her calf. I was on my way to market, but I got held up. I don't know what the boss is going to say about this!' The young, red-haired man shook his head in a daze.

'Never mind that now. We've got to get the cattle out of there.' Fred kept a calm head and looked around for help. 'David, if you're in a fit state, we'll need you to lend a hand.' He took off his old jacket and rolled up his sleeves. 'With a bit of luck, we'll be able to hook the trailer on to a rope and tow it out of the ditch.'

The old farmer had got the rescue operation well underway before anyone else had gathered their wits. He told a bystander to ring the police, then backed his own Land-rover into position at the edge of the ditch. As he threw a rope out to David Moore, a new voice broke through the confusion.

'Eddie!' Footsteps came running down the hill. 'Eddie . . . What the . . . !'

Helen and Hannah saw Terence Cooke stop dead in his tracks at the sight of the damaged trailer. He stood watching David Moore tie the rope round the tow-bar. Then he came racing up.

'Is Highland Lady in there?' He ran and seized the young stockman's arm. 'Is she?' he demanded.

Eddie nodded. He leaned forward to take an end of the rope from David Moore.

The landowner groaned. 'And Skye?'

Another nod.

'Badly hurt?' Cooke asked, running to the far end of the trailer to try to see inside.

'We don't know yet. Now, stand out of the way!' Fred warned.

Forgetting their earlier row, the wealthy farmer obeyed.

'Who's Highland Lady?' Helen sidled up to him and murmured. The landowner seemed genuinely upset.

'She's my prize Highland cow,' he whispered back. 'A real beauty. And the calf is special too. Three months old and already looking like champion material!' His face creased into a deep frown. 'Or was!' he corrected himself. 'Until some idiot drove into them!'

As he looked wildly round for someone to explain what had happened, Helen crept back to stand by Hannah. She told her about the trapped calf.

'That must be Skye!' Hannah watched the men attach the rope to Fred's Land-rover and begin to ease the trailer out of the ditch. Almost drowned by the loud bellowing of the grown cow, she could hear the thin, wailing cry of the calf.

'Steady!' David Moore called. He waved the old farmer forward.

Slowly, inch by inch, they dragged the trailer out. It tilted and rocked, pulled upright, edged forwards.

'Who saw what happened? Who'll be a witness when the police get here?' Terence Cooke demanded. He went up to the group of spectators.

'Not me, mate.'

'Sorry, I never actually saw it.'

'Count me out.' People backed off and shuffled away.

'But they're my prize cows! Pure bred Kyloes from the western isles. Worth a fortune!' He sounded off to anyone who would listen, overlooking Fred's quick-thinking response.

'I thought you said he couldn't be all bad!' Hannah muttered darkly.

'That was when I thought he cared!' Helen realised now that all Cooke was worried about was the money.

'The calf is from the best bull around, by the best cow. Highland Lady has a pedigree as long as your arm!' The landowner caught sight of the blue flashing light of a police car coming up the road. He ran to flag it down. 'That's my prize-winning cow in there!' he yelled at them. 'And the calf; she's a champion too!'

He was beside himself with anger as he dragged the policemen to the scene of the accident.

By this time, Fred had wrenched open the trailer ramp and climbed inside to investigate. Helen and Hannah crept forward, heard the cow shift and bellow from inside.

'She's bleeding badly!' Fred reported. 'It's her front leg!'

'What about the calf?' Hannah asked. She could see the huge cow down on her front knees, her legs awkwardly bent under her, her head straining at the tether. But it was hard to see what lay behind her in the cramped trailer.

'One thing at a time.' Fred called for a rope and a stout stick. 'This cow needs first aid before she bleeds to death!'

Helen ran to their car boot and fetched a tow-rope. Hannah found a stick in the ditch and snapped off its side branches. 'What are you going to do?' she gasped as she handed it to Mr Hunt.

'Make a tourniquet to go around her leg just above the wound,' he explained. His hands were soon covered in blood from the gash above Highland Lady's left knee. But he went on tying the rope to form a noose around the top of the leg. Then he slotted the stick inside the noose and began to twist. Soon the rope tightened and cut off the supply of blood. 'This can stay as it is for a few minutes while someone fetches the vet,' he told them.

'Vet?' Hannah glanced round. Mr Cooke was still yelling, their dad was talking urgently to the stock-man, the policemen were asking the onlookers to be on their way. 'Has anyone rung Mrs Freeman?' she gasped.

'I'll do it!' David Moore volunteered. He ran off to the phone-box.

'How is she?' Helen stared at the injured cow. Mr Hunt was loosening the tether that held her fast. Then he helped her back on to her feet.

'Wait and see,' came Mr Hunt's grunted reply. 'The vet will clean it up and decide what to do.'

Helen noticed that the cow seemed to have quietened down and stopped struggling. She allowed herself to be shunted carefully to one side. But there was a lot of blood on her long, reddish-brown coat and the gash on her leg gaped open.

Behind her, as the farmer gently shifted her, for the first time Helen and Hannah were able to glimpse the tiny calf.

'Poor thing!' Hannah murmured.

The young animal lay on her side. She didn't move, even when her mother stood clear.

'I'm going in to see what's wrong with her!' Helen decided, heaving herself into the trailer and squeezing past Mr Hunt and Highland Lady. 'I can't see any blood,' she reported.

The calf lay blinking up at her as she bent over to examine her frail little body. Beside the adult cow she was skinny and small, her light reddish-gold coat soft and curly. A long, rough fringe of hair almost covered her eyes, so Helen stroked her and gently pushed it back.

'Don't move her!' Fred Hunt suddenly noticed that Helen had climbed into the trailer. 'She may have broken bones, injuries that we can't see!'

'But she needs help!' Hannah cried. It could be ages before Sally Freeman, the vet, arrived.

He nodded. 'We need more space,' he decided.

Judging that it was safe to get Highland Lady out of the trailer, the farmer arranged for the ramp to be lowered. With Edward's help, they led the cow into the open. She hobbled on her injured leg, mooing softly.

Then Fred Hunt turned to the calf. He ran his hands over the small body while Helen stayed by her, soothing her as she lay there, unable to move.

'There, Skye, we'll soon find out what's wrong with you,' she whispered.

'She's broken a bone in this back leg,' Fred said quietly. His broad fingers rested in position. 'I can feel it; a clean break just below the hock.'

Looking in from the ramp, Hannah groaned. 'What should we do?'

'We can try making a temporary splint,' Mr Hunt decided. 'Ask around; see if anyone has a strong, straight piece of wood in the boot of their car!'

'We have!' Hannah immediately thought of the cricket stumps that their dad had fetched from the pavilion a few days earlier, now that the playing season was over. She ran to fetch one and handed it to the business-like farmer.

Mr Cooke noticed her and broke away from his conversation with the policeman. 'What's going on?' he demanded.

'Skye's got a broken leg,' Hannah explained. She watched Mr Hunt strap the cricket stump tight against the calf's leg with the halter rope that Helen had loosened and untied.

'It's a rough job,' Fred admitted, 'but it'll do for now.' He finished tying a firm knot and knelt back with a grunt.

'You're sure it's broken?' Terence Cooke asked angrily, climbing the ramp and standing astride the injured calf. Helen stayed where she was, gently stroking Skye's head, looking up at the tall landowner.

'No doubt about it,' Fred Hunt confirmed. He'd done all he could, so he backed away, out of the trailer. 'She's a young beast, so it should mend nicely, given time. I'd be more worried about the mother if I were you.'

As he gave his verdict, all heads turned to Highland Lady.

The cow had sunk to her knees on the grass verge and collapsed on to her side, her legs stretched out. It looked unnatural and awkward; a sign that she was growing weaker.

'She's lost a lot of blood,' Fred warned. 'And she's suffering from shock.'

Slowly Hannah went over to where the cow lay. She knelt beside her, staring at the blood that still oozed from the large wound, despite Fred's tourniquet.

'What are you saying; that she might die?' Cooke's voice was high and strained, as everyone came and huddled round.

'Wait and see,' the farmer insisted.

But he shook his head as he rolled down his shirt-sleeves. He pulled his cap down over his forehead and reached for his jacket. The frown on his face, the set of his shoulders said more than words as he trudged back to his Land-rover and went on his way.

Three

Half an hour after the crash, Sally Freeman arrived on the scene. She checked Fred Hunt's first-aid, then made rapid arrangements to have Highland Lady and Skye taken back to Coningsby Hall.

'The sooner the better,' she advised, a stethoscope dangling from her neck. 'Both animals are suffering from shock. We need to get them bedded down and treated as fast as we can!'

'Can we go with Mrs Freeman?' Helen asked their dad.

He was busy answering questions for the police, describing how the accident had happened. 'Where to?' He glanced round with a worried frown.

'Up to Coningsby.' Hannah joined Helen to plead with him. 'We've got to go, Dad. We need to find out what happens to Highland Lady and Skye!'

So he nodded, saying he would come as soon as he could. They joined the vet in her car, following Terence Cooke's silver car which now towed the battered trailer carrying the injured cows. Edward would follow shortly in the Land-rover, but first he had to give a statement to the police.

'Why's he going so slowly?' Helen muttered, as the small convoy crept round the steep bends up Rydal Fell.

'He has to take care not to jolt the trailer,' Sally Freeman explained. 'We don't want any further injuries before we get the animals home.'

'How far up the hill is Coningsby?' Hannah asked. She glanced back down into the valley, at Nesfield nestling by the side of Lake Rydal.

'Right over the top, through Snakestone Pass.' Sally drove steadily, concentrating on the narrow, winding road.

'How did Highland Lady seem to you?' Helen gripped a door handle as the car swung round a bend. Up ahead, she saw the trailer sway and tilt.

'Not good,' the vet admitted. 'Sometimes the stress of a sudden shock can be too much for an animal to cope with. And then, of course, she's lost a lot of blood.'

The twins sat in silence, gazing out of the window at the autumn colours on the fellside. The brown heather stretched for miles across the rocky hillsides. The road seemed to go on forever.

'Snakestone Pass!' Hannah breathed at last. The rocks loomed to either side, sending the road zigzagging to find a way through. Mist swirled around them. For a while they lost sight of the trailer ahead.

'Not long now,' Sally Freeman promised.

Then they were over the summit of Rydal Fell and dropping down towards their home village of Doveton. The mist cleared. Ahead of them, they saw the trailer turn off the road, down a sweeping drive.

'Coningsby Hall.' Mrs Freeman pointed out a grand house sheltered by ancient trees. A big 'Keep Out' sign stood at the entrance to the drive.

They saw that the Hall was huge and surrounded by lawns; nothing like the homely, higgledy-piggledy farmhouses they knew. Here, everything was smart new paint, high, clipped hedges, tall windows. Even the barns at the back of the Hall were laid out in an orderly square, around a neatly-swept yard.

'You'd better wait here,' Sally told Hannah and Helen as she drew up alongside Terence Cooke's car.

'Won't you need help?' Hannah asked. She saw Mr Cooke run to the back of the trailer to lower the ramp.

'No, here comes Eddie Huby's Land-rover now. You two should stay where you are.'

A third car pulled up outside the cowshed. They recognised the bashed metal grille and bumper of the Land-rover that had crashed into them, then the wiry, red-headed stockman as he jumped out of the cab.

'Eddie, get over here, quick!' his boss shouted. He and the vet were already lifting Skye down from the trailer and carrying her into the barn.

Helen and Hannah saw only her furry brown head, her splinted leg amidst the rush of activity. They heard her call faintly for her mother. Then she disappeared into the darkness of the huge stone building.

Seconds ticked by. The twins waited, nerves on edge, listening to every sound.

'It's very quiet inside the trailer!' Hannah whispered. She drew the zip of her jacket up to her neck to keep out the cold wind. It had begun to drizzle steadily.

Highland Lady was still in there, they knew. 'Let's take a look!' Helen said.

They crept forward, hearing urgent voices inside the barn. Still silence from the trailer.

'Oh no!' Hannah peered in. The mother cow lay on her side, her eyes closed. She was perfectly still.

Helen gasped and ran for the vet. 'You've got to come!' she shouted, running down a central aisle between two rows of pens. Her footsteps echoed on the stone floor. Inside their stalls, the cattle stirred restlessly. 'Please! It's Highland Lady!'

Sally Freeman grabbed her bag and left Skye with Eddie and his boss. She ran back to the yard with Helen. 'Stay out!' she ordered the twins as she scrambled into the trailer.

They stood in the cold rain and watched as she sounded the cow's heart, then felt for a pulse at the base of her neck. She re-positioned the stethoscope and listened again. Her head dropped for a second, then she looked up.

'Too late?' Hannah whispered.

'I'm afraid so.' Mrs Freeman stood up and came quietly out of the trailer. She put a hand on Hannah's shoulder and delivered the awful news. 'She was already dead. There was nothing I could do.'

'Skye *is* going to get better, isn't she?' Helen ran up to Eddie Huby the moment he emerged from the barn.

Sally Freeman had bolted the trailer door with Highland Lady still inside and gone back to help with the calf. Long minutes dragged by. Then the stockman came out into the yard.

'The vet's setting the bone into position now,' he reported. He steered away from the trailer, out towards the fields at the back of the hall, hanging his head as he went.

Helen and Hannah trailed after him.

'I've had my fill of problems for one week,' the farmhand sighed. He leaned on the fence and studied a small herd of Highland cattle grazing there. 'On Monday I hear that the boss wants to sell off most of the herd. Out of the blue; no warning. Today, Thursday, I crash his new trailer and kill his prize cow.' He shook his head in disbelief.

Hannah and Helen stood beside him in silence, watching the cattle move slowly and quietly through the misty rain. They ducked their huge heads to graze. Their great, curved horns almost scraped the ground.

'What do they say: trouble comes in threes?' Eddie Huby dug the toe of his boot into the soft earth. 'Next thing I know, Mr Cooke will be handing me my notice. I'll be out of a job by the end of the week, just you wait!'

Helen and Hannah heard Eddie's words but their minds were still on the injured calf. They stared at the strange, slow-moving cattle and didn't even recognise the sound of their father's car as it came down the drive to the Hall. They only started out of their daze when voices were raised in the yard.

'What's that?' Helen jerked her head round.

'It sounds like Dad!' Hannah turned and headed off. 'Come on!'

'Why is Mr Cooke yelling at him?' Helen caught her up. As they turned the corner, they saw the two men standing face to face by the barn door.

'. . . Brand new trailer!' the landowner shouted. His face was red, he waved his arms wildly. 'Not to mention the damage to my stockman's Land-rover!'

The girls skidded to a halt beside their father.

'I'm not taking the blame for this,' David Moore said firmly. He didn't shout or lose his temper, but he wouldn't give way. 'I didn't do anything wrong!'

'You call crossing a red light doing nothing wrong!'

'I didn't cross a red light.'

The angry landowner leaned in even closer. 'I

have witnesses to say that you did!' he claimed. David Moore's calmness only seemed to infuriate him more. 'And then there's the value of the cattle!' he went on, more and more red in the face. 'Highland Lady was worth thousands! And the calf. I won't be able to sell her for a decent price now that her leg's broken! I won't get anything like what she's worth!'

'I'm sorry about your cows,' David admitted. 'No one likes to see animals suffer.'

Hannah heard footsteps come up behind them. She turned to appeal to Eddie Huby. 'Tell Mr Cooke what happened!' she whispered. After all, Eddie had been the one who'd skipped the red light as he flew down the hill.

But the stockman shoved his hands in his pockets, blushed bright-red and walked on by.

Hannah stared at his disappearing back, about to follow and drag him back. But Helen held her arm. 'Listen!' she hissed.

' . . . And then there's the vet's bills!' Cooke shouted. 'They won't be cheap. This whole business is going to cost a fortune.'

David Moore had heard enough. He cleared

his throat and shook his head. 'We'll talk about
this when you've calmed down.'

'Oh no!' The landowner stepped in front of him
again as he tried to walk away. 'We'll talk about it
now. You'll cough up what you owe me, or else!'

'Or else what?' The challenge went back, firm
and steady.

Cooke fumed. He spat out his final furious words.
'Or else, Moore, I'll take you to court. I warn you, I
will. I'll sue you for every penny you've got!'

Four

'Every penny we've got won't get him very far!' David Moore gave a hollow laugh as he gave his wife the news.

The twins' mother managed a faint smile. She let Socks, the Home Farm cat, snuggle up on her knee as she put her feet up by the fire. It had been a hard day's work at the Curlew Cafe and she really didn't need this. 'Perhaps Mr Cooke didn't mean it,' she said wearily.

'Oh, he meant it, didn't he, girls?' Their dad sat forward in his chair and rested his elbows on his knees.

35

Hannah nodded. 'He was pretty mad.'

'And *he's* the one who ought to be sorry!' Helen protested. She drew the curtains to shut out the dark, wet night, then settled on a floor cushion next to Speckle, their black-and-white Border collie.

'It was his stockman who drove into *us*!' Hannah went on.

'We could have been hurt!'

'Or killed!'

'Now, Hannah, don't exaggerate,' Mary Moore said kindly.

'Highland Lady *was* killed,' Helen pointed out.

There was silence for a while as they all stared at the flames in the hearth.

'In any case, if Mr Cooke does go ahead and sue us, how much would it be likely to cost?' Mary Moore got down to the facts.

David shrugged. He began a list on his fingers. 'A couple of hundred pounds to fix the Land-rover. A lot more to repair the trailer, I expect.'

'How much more?'

'Maybe five or six hundred.'

Hannah's eyebrows shot up. This sounded like an awful lot of money.

'Then there's Highland Lady,' their dad said quietly.

'He said she was worth thousands,' Helen muttered.

'Thousands!' Mary Moore sat up in her seat, tipping Socks to the floor. The little cat stretched and padded off to the kitchen to look for her supper.

'Highland Lady was a prize-winning, pure-bred Kyloe.' Hannah could remember Cooke's description, word for word. 'And Skye's supposed to be a champion in the making.'

Their mum frowned. 'Well, we can't afford that kind of money,' she said, looking round the room. 'Even if we sold everything we possess, we wouldn't be able to pay him what he's asking!'

Hannah and Helen followed her gaze. There was the lumpy old sofa covered with colourful throws, the small TV, the broken video. The family didn't have a lot of money, though their mum worked hard in her cafe and their dad earned as much as he could taking wildlife photographs for magazines.

'I suppose we could sell the car to pay our debts if we lose,' Mary said, looking on the gloomy side for once.

'Have you seen it since it was in the crash?' David asked with a wry grin. 'The driver's door doesn't open and the front bumper is hanging on by a thread . . .'

She threw up her hands. 'Don't go on!'

Helen stroked Speckle thoughtfully. 'What will happen if we do lose and we can't pay?'

'We won't lose,' David Moore said, putting another log on the fire.

'But if we do?' Hannah insisted.

'Hmm.' He sat down again with a groan. 'Well, if it came to it, and the court really did think it was my fault, I suppose we'd have to sell the house.'

'Sell Home Farm?' Helen echoed. She and Hannah were out in the barn giving Solo fresh hay and water. The pony was in his stall, out of the wind and rain.

'What would happen to Solo then?' Hannah murmured, laying her cheek against his warm, strong neck.

'And the geese and the hens, and . . . and!' Helen turned around under the high, dark roof. She thought of all the animals who crowded happily together in the barn, the farmyard and the field here at Home Farm.

'We've got to help Dad!' Hannah declared. She stuffed hay into Solo's net and hitched it on to the hook.

'We'll give evidence in court!' Helen decided. 'We'll be witnesses. Tell them the accident wasn't his fault!'

'Will they believe us?' Hannah didn't know exactly who 'they' would be. She pictured a judge in a long wig, a row of men and women in the jury box.

'It's the truth!'

'Yes, but . . .' Hannah didn't think they could afford to wait until then. They had to do something sooner. 'Listen, we know Mum and Dad can't afford to fight Mr Cooke.'

'And they can't afford to give in and pay him what he wants either.' Helen splashed water from the hose into Solo's bucket. The pony drank noisily as they made their plan.

'So we have to find our own witnesses.' Suddenly everything became clear to Hannah. Her face brightened as she took a brush from the tack shelf and began to groom Solo.

'Who?' Helen stopped to think.

'Well, there's Mr Hunt for a start.'

'And the people in the car behind us. They stopped to see what happened next, remember!' Now Helen grew excited. She thought of the little knot of onlookers who must have seen the crash, then paused. 'Do we know who they were?'

'No, but we could ask in town.' Hannah was determined to go ahead. 'Tomorrow's Friday. No school because it's still half-term. So let's set off early!'

Helen nodded. 'But let's not tell Mum and Dad.'

'Why not?'

'We don't want to get their hopes up, do we?'

'OK,' Hannah agreed. 'We'll take Speckle across to High Hartwell to see Mr Hunt.'

As the twins finished their work in the barn, switched off the light and crossed the yard towards the cosy farmhouse, they felt better. They had a secret plan, and their hopes were high that tomorrow morning they would persuade the honest old farmer to be the star witness in their case against the dreaded *Lord* Terence Cooke!

*

'You'll find him in the cowshed; where else?' Fred's wife, Hilda, greeted Hannah and Helen from the front door of High Hartwell.

Seth, the thin sheepdog who guarded the gate, had warned her that she had visitors. Now the farm cat, Tom, came stalking from the house.

'He's busy admiring his two new weanlings,' Hilda warned them with a laugh. 'When he had our children about the place, he never spent half so much time on them as he does on his precious calves!'

So they jogged across the yard, into the warm, muggy barn, searching for Fred between the rows of empty stalls. Except for the new youngsters, his herd of Friesians were out on the sloping pasture below the farm, grazing the last of the year's growth before winter set in.

'Mr Hunt!' Helen's eager voice echoed in the high space. Their footsteps sounded loud and clear.

'Over here,' he grunted, standing up suddenly in a pen where he kept his prized youngsters. 'What brings you over here so early on a Friday morning?' he asked suspiciously. 'Why aren't you at school?'

'Holiday!' Hannah said cheerily. She climbed on

a wooden bar to lean over and stroke the nearest calf. The patches of black on her back looked like a map of the world, she decided.

'Well, you're too late to help with the milking,' he grumbled. 'So what can I do for you?'

'It's about yesterday,' Helen began. She climbed up alongside Hannah. 'The crash.'

'Mmm. Bad business,' he growled. 'I heard the cow died.'

'And did you hear that Mr Cooke's blaming Dad?' Hannah took over from Helen.

'I heard something of the sort.' Mr Hunt made

himself busy again, pouring calf nuts into a shallow trough and letting the calves feed. 'He's that type of man; thinks he knows it all, never listens.' He dismissed the landowner with a shrug. 'Not my cup of tea at all.'

'But you know it wasn't really Dad's fault, don't you?' Hannah built up to the real question. Behind her back, she kept her fingers firmly crossed.

The farmer grunted and watched the calves.

'You saw Eddie Huby jump the red light and drive right into us!' Helen pressed the point home. Now it all came out in a rush. 'We need you to tell everyone what you saw, so Mr Cooke can't blame Dad and take him to court. Then we won't have to pay for all the damage, and he can't sue us and we won't lose Home Farm!' she gabbled.

'Now hold on just a minute!' Fred Hunt turned slowly and rested his arms along the top bar of the stall. He tipped his cap back from his forehead. 'Did you say "court"?'

Hannah nodded. 'Mr Cooke's going to sue us for every penny we've got!' She repeated the phrase that had burnt into her memory. 'We want you to be our witness!'

'I don't know.' The old man shook his head. 'I'm not one for going to court. It always ends up costing money.' His low voice rumbled and growled slowly on as he pondered the situation.

'But it wouldn't cost you anything to be a witness!' Hannah protested. 'You'd just have to say that you saw Mr Huby jump the lights and drive straight into us!'

'Ah!' He held up a gnarled finger and wagged it. 'That's just the point, see. I didn't *see* it.'

'Didn't . . . ?'

'See it!' Helen's face fell. 'How come?'

'I was ahead of you, well past the lights when it happened, remember.'

Hannah's mouth had dried up. She swallowed hard and her voice came out as a croak. 'But didn't you see it in your mirror?'

Fred shook his head. 'I was looking at the road ahead. By the time I heard the smash and used the mirror, it was all over. I stopped as soon as I could and ran back to see what I could do to help, of course. But no, I never actually saw what happened!'

'Couldn't you *say* you did?' Helen pleaded. Fred Hunt had been their main hope.

'That'd be a lie.' He shook his head again, then turned back to attend to his calves. 'No, much as I dislike Terence Cooke, and much as I'd like to help your mum and dad out of a tight spot, you can see how it is. I can't possibly be your witness in court.'

'Oh!' Hannah gave way to her disappointment. She jumped down from the bar and slumped against the nearby wall. 'What are we going to do now?'

Helen turned and walked off, unable to speak.

'Well, you're not going to give in just like that!' The farmer's deep voice called after them.

They stopped to listen.

'What's one little setback?' he insisted. 'It's nothing to a couple of smart young lasses like you two.'

They squared their shoulders.

He's right! Hannah thought.

'Of course!' Helen said to herself.

'It's true that I can't help,' Fred told them. 'But what you do now is go right out there and find someone who can! '

Five

'Plan number two!' Helen announced.

She and Hannah stood on the doorstep of Honeysuckle Cottage, a guest-house looking over the shores of Lake Rydal.

Hannah rang the bell and waited. 'If I have to keep my fingers crossed for much longer, they'll get stuck!' she muttered.

Their search for a witness to the crash had brought them from High Hartwell, across to Nesfield with their dad. While David Moore had taken the car to the garage for repairs, the twins had been playing detective.

'We've come about the crash at the traffic lights that happened yesterday morning,' Hannah had told the police officer on duty at the town police station.

'Ye-es?' The young woman behind the desk had been suspicious at first. 'If you want to offer us information, it's a bit late. We've already got all the witnesses we need, thank you.'

'It's the witnesses we've come about,' Helen had explained eagerly. 'Where do they live?'

'Why do you want to know?'

'We want to tell them what happened to the cows in the trailer,' Hannah had said, blushing slightly.

'I hear one died?' The policewoman was up-to-date with the news.

Helen had nodded. 'We want to tell the people who watched the rescue. Do you know where they're staying, please?'

'There were several people on the spot, but the two we took statements from are tourists.' The woman had looked up the file. 'I suppose it won't do any harm for you to speak to them. Their name is Kirk; Mr and Mrs. You should find them at Honeysuckle Cottage on Lakeside.'

So here they were, waiting for the landlady to

answer the door, peering through frosted glass at a stout shape approaching down the hallway.

Hannah squeezed her fingers tightly into the crossed position.

'Could we speak to Mr and Mrs Kirk, please?' Helen said brightly.

'You could . . .' the landlady began. She smiled kindly at the two anxious, identical faces surrounded by dark, bobbed hair and long, straight fringes.

Helen's heart raced. Hannah took a sharp intake of breath.

' . . . Except that they're not here.' The landlady shook her head, sorry to disappoint them.

'Not here?' Helen echoed.

'No, they packed up and left for Manchester early this morning. It was the end of their holiday. Sorry, dear.'

The door closed quietly.

'So much for plan number two,' Helen sighed. She turned and gazed out over the misty lake at the mountains on the far shore. 'What's plan number three, then?'

'Eddie Huby,' Hannah said the name of Terence

Cooke's stockman with quiet determination.

They'd met up with their dad at the garage and come home for lunch. David Moore hadn't been his usual cheerful self as he drove over Snakestone Pass, past Coningsby Hall. The bill to repair the car door had been much more than he'd expected, and money worries weighed him down. 'If Mr Cooke carries on blaming me, we're in real trouble,' he'd said again, as he set their lunch of soup and crusty bread on the kitchen table and left them to it.

'Eddie Huby . . . what?' Helen asked. She chewed her bread listlessly, wondering what Hannah was up to now.

'Think about it. Eddie Huby is the only other person who really knows what happened yesterday.' Hannah had been thinking about this on the long drive home.

'So?' Helen pushed her soup around the bowl with her spoon.

'So, we've got to get him to tell the truth!'

'Just like that?' Sometimes Hannah didn't think straight. Helen slurped her soup to show her that the idea wasn't worth considering.

'Why not?' Hannah insisted.

'Because he won't help, will he?'

'Why not?'

'Because *Lord* Terence Cooke is his boss, that's why not!' Noisily Helen scraped the bottom of her bowl.

'So?'

'So, we already know that Eddie Huby's scared of his boss!'

Hannah sat in silence, staring at her own soup. 'Have you got a better idea?' she asked through gritted teeth.

'Git on!' Eddie Huby growled, waving his arms wide and herding a group of cows into the barn at Coningsby Hall.

The square, long-haired Highland cattle barged and jostled each other through the door.

'Go on, git on!' he called, tapping a rump with a long, light stick, waving his arms until the last one had disappeared from the yard.

'Plan number three!' Helen breathed.

Against her better judgment, she'd agreed to try Hannah's plan. They'd cycled over from Home Farm that same afternoon, dumped their bikes in a ditch

51

outside the main gates and sneaked around to the back of the Hall, lying in wait for a glimpse of the stockman going about his business on the farm.

'Come on!' Hannah was eager to go and talk to Eddie. She would reason with him, point out the facts, make him see sense . . .

'What if Mr Cooke sees us?' Helen put out a hand to hold Hannah back. 'His car's here, remember!'

They'd spotted the sleek silver saloon out at the front of the house, by the broad stone steps.

And it was a good job that Helen had reminded Hannah, for the landowner came out of a back door as she spoke, striding across the yard, checking this and that with his beady eyes.

Hannah and Helen ducked down behind a wall, their hearts thumping.

'Why does he always look so angry?' Helen whispered. Mr Cooke's face wore a permanent frown.

Hannah took a deep breath, then peered over the wall-top in time to see the tall figure disappear inside the barn. She listened hard to what the boss was telling his stockman.

'I thought I told you, no milk feed for Skye from

now on!' Cooke shouted from one end of the barn to the other.

Eddie Huby's reply was too quiet for them to hear, but his boss wasn't listening in any case.

'No milk feed after a calf reaches eight weeks; you know that perfectly well. And go easy on the calf nuts. She's not going to be running about with the others with that broken leg of hers, is she?'

'Mean thing!' Helen breathed, peering over the wall with Hannah.

They both ducked again as Terence Cooke reappeared in the doorway. He was wagging his finger at Eddie, who appeared with him, sleeves rolled back, waistcoat hanging open.

'I think we should bring the vet back,' the stockman insisted in a worried voice as they walked across the yard. 'I'm still not happy about her.'

'What's the matter? The leg's set right, isn't it?' Cooke brushed off the concern.

'Yes. It's not the leg. It's her general condition. She's only a youngster, and she's lost her mother, remember. I think the shock of that could set her back a long way.'

'Poor Skye!' Hannah whispered.

'And what good would the vet do?' Cooke insisted. 'It would just cost me more money, that's all.'

The two men passed close to where the twins were hidden, cutting down the side of the house and making their way around to the front.

' . . . Better safe than sorry . . . just a check over . . . really not happy . . .' The stockman's voice tailed off.

They heard the landowner give a sharp, final reply. Then a car door opened and shut and there was the sound of an engine starting up. Wheels crunched over gravel as the car drew away.

'Come on!' Helen whispered. She put a foot on a jutting out stone in the wall and began to climb over.

'To the barn?' Hannah was already alongside her.

Helen nodded and jumped into the yard. 'To see Skye!'

They couldn't bear to think of her, sad and lonely, with her leg set in stiff, uncomfortable plaster, missing her mother.

So they ventured into the barn, with its hosed concrete floor, its rows of metal stalls. The cattle there raised their enormous brown heads from their mangers as the twins passed. They shook their

shaggy fringes and stamped their enormous hooves.

'There's Skye!' Hannah pointed out the small, injured heifer. She was in a stall in the far corner of the barn, poking her head through the rails and making a blowing, bleating sound as they went up.

'*Blaa-aah!*' She blew noisily and tossed her head. Her soft pink muzzle stretched out through the bars.

Helen went forward to stroke her matted forehead and soft, round ears. Hannah watched the calf totter half a step, trailing the stiff broken leg behind.

'All alone!' Helen whispered. 'We know; it's very sad!'

The calf gave out her distressed, snorting call. '*Blaa-aah!*'

Hannah reached in to stroke her too. 'You'll soon feel better,' she promised. It made her feel angry that Cooke had refused to send for Sally Freeman again.

The calf licked and nudged their hands, desperate for attention. And they were so busy trying to calm and soothe her that they didn't notice when a side door opened, casting a narrow shaft of daylight across the floor of the barn. Only when footsteps rang out across the concrete floor did they look up to see Eddie Huby striding towards them.

'Now, just hold on!' His voice echoed and he held up a warning hand for them not to run off.

Helen and Hannah froze to the spot.

'Who said you two could come in here?' The stockman frowned down at them, hands on hips, blocking their escape route. 'This is private property!'

Hannah swallowed hard. 'We came to see how Skye was.'

He studied her anxious face and seemed to relent. 'It's a good job Mr Cooke didn't catch you. He'd have sent you packing, believe me.'

Hannah nodded. 'Will we get you into trouble?'

'No, you're all right.' Eddie Huby jerked his head in the direction of the house. 'The boss has just gone off into town for the afternoon.'

'How is Skye, really?' Helen still had one hand on the calf's flank. She could feel her trembling underneath her thick, shaggy coat.

'Not so good.' Eddie drew the bolt and let the door of the stall swing open. 'She's off her feed, and I've had instructions not to give her milk.' He gazed at Skye, then patted her. 'That's a mistake in my opinion, but I've been given my orders!'

'Doesn't Mr Cooke care about her?' Hannah asked. She could see that the stockman was genuinely worried.

'I wouldn't say he doesn't care. After all, this is a champion heifer we're talking about here.' Eddie coaxed Skye out of the pen so that he could muck it out. 'Kiward!' he urged, offering the calf his fingers to suck.

'What does that mean?' Helen heard the curious word, spoken gently.

' "Kiward"?' He grinned. 'It means, "get a move

on" when you're leading from in front. If you're behind the beast, "Git on!" is what you say.'

Slowly Skye edged out of the stall, keeping the weight off her broken leg. Eddie slipped a halter round her neck and gave it to Helen to hold.

'I'll help you muck out!' Hannah offered, taking a rake from a nearby hook and beginning to clear the straw from the floor. Between them, she and the stockman made a new bed for Skye.

'You mustn't be too hard on the boss,' Eddie said after a while. He leaned on his rake and tried to make them understand. 'He's got personal problems just now, but he's not always like this.'

'You mean, he does like his cows, after all?' Helen sounded unconvinced.

Eddie nodded. 'He's a real expert on these Highland cattle, knows all there is to know. They're strong, thrifty, hardy beasts. They can live on next to nothing where they come from in the highlands of Scotland. And they're lovely looking.' The stockman spoke with pride about his boss's herd. 'But it makes no economic sense to breed them.'

'What do you mean?' Hannah asked. She was warm from working in the stall. She liked Eddie

Huby, she decided. His freckled face was open and friendly under his shock of wavy red hair.

'I mean, the boss would make a lot more money from rearing Friesians or most other breeds of cow. But it's not the profit he can make that matters in the end. It's the fact that he loves his Kyloes.'

Eddie put his head to one side, then seemed to make a decision. 'Come on, let's get Skye bedded down, then I can show you something.' He asked Helen to lead the calf gently and slowly into the clean stall. Then he closed and bolted the door and gave her a final pat.

'Where are we going?' Hannah ran to catch up with him as he strode down the length of the barn. To either side, the cattle mooed and shifted in their stalls.

'This way!' Eddie led them out into the yard and across the square of barn buildings to another, smaller wing. 'It's not only champion cattle that Mr Cooke breeds.'

'What else?' Helen stepped after him into the next barn. It was lighter, airier. Sunlight poured in through the open doors. She could see tiers of wooden roosting-poles, rows of square nesting-boxes lined with straw – and hens.

Round, gleaming hens of all colours clucking and scurrying freely across the floor. Speckled hens darting their heads at grain and pecking with sharp beaks. Black hens with red combs scratching in the dust. White hens with strange, soft feathery legs and tails.

'Those are Silkies,' Eddie told them, following their silent gaze. 'And the other ones with feathered legs over there are White Cochins. Those are Silver-laced Wyandottes, and that chap up there with the golden head is a Faverolle!'

The strange names rolled off his tongue, leaving the twins open-mouthed. The whole barn was alive with exotic breeds of hens. Downy feathers drifted down from the perches where hens pecked and groomed. Soft cooing noises came from the broody ones in their nesting boxes.

' . . . Dark Cuckoo Marans . . . Anconas . . . Old English Game . . .' Eddie's list went on. He beamed at the twins' astonished faces. 'They're Mr Cooke's pride and joy, these hens. And every one is a champion!'

Six

'And the star of them all is Oscar!'

Eddie pointed to the large, brightly-coloured cockerel perched high in the barn. He was the bird with the golden head and neck. His wings were red, his chest and tail feathers black. When he saw them gazing up at him, he puffed out his chest, raised his scarlet comb and crowed.

'What make is he?' Helen had forgotten the exotic name.

'You mean breed? He's a Faverolle. Look at the feathers on his legs. They're like spurs!' Eddie chuckled at the boastful bird, who turned, chest still puffed out, and began to strut along his high pole. Sunlight caught the golden head feathers and made them glint, then he stretched his red wings and fluttered to the ground.

The hens scattered as he landed.

'See that Ancona run!' Eddie laughed at a small green hen who scuttled out of the cockerel's way. 'Oscar's the boss around here, make no mistake!'

'They're funny!' Hannah had begun to smile.

'And beautiful,' Helen added. Their own hens, in the yard at Home Farm, were the common brown, speckled kind. As far as she knew, they didn't have fancy names like Faverolles and Anconas. Here there were hens with lovely black-and-white markings, like patterns in lace, and tiny black bantams with long, curved tail feathers.

'Some of these breeds are pretty rare,' Eddie told them. 'That means they're worth a lot.'

'Of course,' Hannah muttered. At Coningsby Hall, so much of the talk seemed to be about money.

Eddie seemed to read her thoughts. 'But that's not the point,' he insisted. 'All the hens here lay free-range eggs. It's the old-fashioned way; more natural but less efficient. It means they can come

and go as they please into the field at the back. We just shut them in at night to guard against foxes and suchlike.'

'So you don't get as many eggs to sell?' Helen liked this idea better than keeping hens cooped up twenty-four hours a day. She knew too that her mum was careful to buy free-range eggs for the cafe.

The stockman nodded. 'What I'm getting at is, the boss doesn't put profit before everything else, no matter what you might think.'

'Then why won't he send for the vet for Skye?' Hannah asked.

'You heard that, did you? I can't give you an answer to that, I'm afraid.' Eddie shrugged and walked them over to look at a large box lit by an infra-red lamp. The box was lined with corrugated cardboard, and woodshavings were spread over the floor.

'Chicks!' Helen leaned over the box to see the tiny yellow birds. They were soft and yellow, and hopped awkwardly on their orange legs.

But Hannah wasn't going to be softened up by the sweet, fluffy chicks. She remembered the reason why they'd come. 'Yes, and the other question I wanted to ask is, why has Mr Cooke got it in for our dad?'

'How do you mean?' The farmhand's pale, freckled skin coloured up easily. He grunted and poured a fresh supply of special chick crumbs into the drum-shaped feeder for the young birds.

'Why is he blaming us for the accident yesterday?' Hannah turned her back and stared at Oscar, who strutted the length of the barn to be admired by the hens.

Helen filled the silence. 'Haven't you told him that it wasn't our fault?'

Eddie cleared his throat. Refusing to look at them, he went off to fetch water for the chicks. 'There's no point,' he muttered. 'Mr Cooke wouldn't listen. That's the sort of mood he's in at the moment.'

'You could try,' Hannah said quietly. She and Helen followed in his footsteps as he went back to the brooder. 'If you told him the accident was your fault, he'd have to stop blaming Dad, wouldn't he?'

They stared in at the chicks gathered round the feeder, tails in the air, beaks pecking hungrily.

'Yes, and I'd lose my job,' Eddie said quietly.

Helen gasped. 'You mean he'd sack you if he knew you'd jumped the light?'

He nodded. 'It's on my conscience, what he's threatening to do to your father. But I'm in a tight spot here. I was coming down the hill into town pretty fast, I admit. But I'd been held up. I was late getting the cattle to market and I knew what a bad mood the boss would be in because of it. So I was in a hurry, and may just have skipped the lights . . .'

On either side of him, Helen and Hannah looked up and nodded.

' . . . But it's more than my job's worth to own up,' he said again.

Hannah sighed. 'So you won't help us?'

'Even if it means Dad has to go to court?' Helen asked.

Eddie Huby broke away and strode out into the yard. 'I'm sorry,' he muttered.

With sinking hearts they watched him walk across the yard. Then he paused by the side of the house and listened. A car was coming down the drive, its wheels crunching over the gravel. Hannah and Helen heard him groan and head back towards them. 'You'd better get out of here as quick as you can,' he warned.

'Why? Is that Mr Cooke's car?' Helen remembered their bikes hidden in the ditch by the gate. They would have to return that way to collect them.

'No, it's his wife's. I recognise the sound of the engine. I wonder what she's doing here.' The stockman seemed not to know which way to turn.

'Doesn't she live here?' Hannah asked. Come to think of it, it was the first time anyone had mentioned a Mrs Cooke.

'Not any more. A week ago, she and the boss had a big argument. She left home, went to live in town and hasn't been back since!' There was panic in his eyes. 'If he comes home early and finds her here, there'll be an almighty row!'

'Why don't you go and warn her?' Helen took in the news. No wonder Terence Cooke had been in such a bad mood lately. She tried to imagine Mrs Cooke; probably a smart woman with blonde hair.

But while Eddie dithered, the car crunched to a halt. There were light footsteps coming towards them, and before Hannah and Helen could make themselves scarce, they found out for a fact what the landowner's wife looked like.

'She's not going into the house, she's coming round here!' Eddie yelped.

'Eddie!' A woman came round the corner and called his name. Her short hair was light brown. She wasn't smart, but dressed for the autumn weather in a green waxed jacket, trousers and boots.

The twins stood awkwardly outside the henhouse door. Oscar the cockerel came strutting in front of them, fixing his bright black eye on the newcomer and showing off as before. Hannah and Helen felt it was only a matter of time before they got thrown out. But they needn't have worried. Mrs Cooke ignored the visitors and went straight up to the stockman.

'What's this I hear about Highland Lady and Skye?' she asked breathlessly. 'I was in town this afternoon when I heard. Is it true, Lady was killed?'

Eddie hung his head and nodded.

'That's dreadful! How has Terence taken it?'

'Pretty bad.'

'And what about little Skye? How is she? Is her leg really broken?'

Eddie told her that it was all true, and Mrs Cooke,

on the verge of tears, rushed to see the injured calf. As she ran past the twins, Oscar got in the way and almost managed to trip her.

'What were they doing in the trailer in the first place?' she asked, as she shooed the cockerel to one side and rushed on into the cowshed. 'Where were you taking them?'

'To market.' Eddie followed more slowly, standing back as Mrs Cooke went and made a fuss of the calf.

'To market?' She repeated his words with a shake of her head. 'You mean, Terence was sending Skye and Lady into Nesfield to sell them? What on earth for?'

'Search me.' Eddie grew more and more uncomfortable under cross-questioning from the boss's wife. He shifted his feet and stared at the ground, unaware of the twins still hovering in the background.

'But he doesn't sell his prize cattle without a good reason!' She petted Skye and looked at her splinted leg. 'Anyway, Lady and Skye actually belong to me!' The more she thought about recent events, the more upset she became. 'What's he up to, Eddie?'

There was no time for him to search for a satisfactory answer. A second car was speeding down the drive. It didn't stop by the house, but drove straight round the side and into the yard. The twins saw the long, silver bonnet and started to run.

'Hold it!' Cooke slammed on the brakes, jumped out of the car and yelled after them.

They stopped. They didn't dare to move a muscle at the sound of his angry voice.

As soon as he heard his boss's car, Eddie seemed to vanish into thin air. Next time Helen and Hannah looked round, he was nowhere to be seen.

'One almighty row coming up!' Helen whispered.

Mrs Cooke came running out of the cowshed. 'How dare you send my cattle to market?' she demanded, her jacket flapping open in the wind, her red silk scarf whipped across her cheek. 'They're mine, not yours! You had no business to even consider selling them!'

'Says who?' Cooke had spotted her car and prepared for battle. Now he stood his ground. 'You gave up all your rights over the livestock here the moment you walked out!' he yelled back. 'So don't come here trying to tell me what to do!'

'You're outrageous, Terence! But you won't get away with it. I've been to see my solicitor!'

'Hah!' The landowner's laugh was cruel, his voice was a spiteful sneer. 'By the time any solicitor gets his act together, it'll be too late!'

Helen frowned at Hannah. 'Too late?'

'Shh!' Hannah shook her head and tried to listen.

'What do you mean? You're not to touch the livestock on this farm!' Mrs Cooke's voice rose to a shriek. 'Are you listening to me, Terence? Legally, you're not allowed to sell a single animal or bird without my agreement! And if you do, I'll . . . I'll!' Words failed her as she glared down at Oscar, who had come strutting through the narrow gap between her and her angry husband.

He didn't flinch. He let her come to within a few inches of him without batting an eyelid. 'Too late,' he said again, quiet and sinister. 'I've just been into town and found buyers for the entire herd.'

Seven

Terence Cooke had spelled it out a second time outside the barn at Coningsby Hall for his wife to understand; 'By this time next week there won't be a single beast left here!'

'Looks like he meant it,' Helen said miserably. It was Saturday morning and they were standing with Speckle outside the Curlew Cafe, watching Eddie Huby tow a trailer into Nesfield town square. Mr Cooke himself followed in a second Land-rover, with another trailer. As they parked and waited nearby, the twins could see two shaggy, horned heads peering out of the back of each.

Hannah got the point. 'He's selling the cattle,' she said sadly. 'He really is going ahead.'

' . . . To spite his wife.'

' . . . Even though he cares about them.' She shook her head and gazed at the huge cows cooped up in the trailers. As their tousled heads turned, their horns clashed and drew a small crowd of admirers.

'Look at them!' a boy stared up from a safe distance, half in awe.

'Wow! They're so . . . big!' his friend breathed.

But a poker-faced Mr Cooke came and asked them to stand to one side while he let down the ramp of the first trailer. Helen and Hannah saw that the cattle were securely tethered in their straw-lined box.

'Where's Grindleford got to?' the landowner grumbled, checking his watch. 'The town square is where we arranged to meet; halfway between Coningsby and his place over at Melham. I told him to be here at eight-thirty, sharp.'

Eddie Huby shrugged. He settled down to wait with a glum expression, pretending that he hadn't seen the twins.

'What's wrong with you?' Cooke said sharply, objecting to the stockman's silence. 'I'm selling the

74

beasts on to a decent owner, aren't I?' He seemed to be speaking in a loud voice, especially so that the twins could overhear, though he too had ignored them up till now.

'I didn't say a word.' Eddie stuck his hands in his pockets and stared up at the heavy, grey sky.

'No, but I can tell what you're thinking. You don't want me to sell them. But Grindleford is a specialist breeder with a good reputation. They're going to a decent home.'

'That's fine for these four.' Eddie spoke up at last. 'But what about the rest? They'll be split up and sold to any Tom, Dick or Harry.'

His boss turned away with an impatient grunt. Once more he looked at his watch. 'Wait here,' he told Eddie. 'I'm going to take a look up Market Street, to see if Grindleford is on his way.'

Cooke glared at Hannah and Helen as he stamped off. They waited until he was well out of sight before they began to sidle over to the trailers for a peek at the cattle.

'Helen-Hannah, don't go far!' their mum warned from inside the cafe. 'I need you to run an errand for me!'

'It's OK, we won't be long,' Hannah called back, sending Speckle into the cafe. She and Helen couldn't resist one last close look at the Kyloes.

'You two never learn, do you?' Eddie muttered a warning. 'If the boss catches you, he won't be very happy.'

As soon as the row between him and his wife had died down the day before, Mr Cooke had sent the twins on their way. 'I don't want you anywhere near these beasts!' he'd yelled. Adding, for good measure, 'Or setting foot on my property ever again. Is that clear?'

So Helen promised the stockman that they only wanted to sneak a quick glance. 'How's Skye?' she asked quietly, peering in at the restless cows.

He sniffed. 'Still in a lot of pain, if you ask me. I'm wondering if the leg's been set right after all.'

'But Mr Cooke still won't call Mrs Freeman?' Hannah asked.

'No, he's too busy getting his own back against Mrs Cooke to pay the calf any attention. And she's pining for her mother, I can tell.' He paused as he frowned down at the cobbles. 'The worst of it is, far from being the champion little heifer that she was before the accident, she's now worse than useless.'

'How come?' Helen kept an eye on the entrance to Market Street, in case Terence Cooke came stomping back.

'Well, if the leg doesn't heal properly and she loses weight through not eating, who's going to want to buy her?' Eddie made it as plain as he could. 'And if the boss can't find a buyer for her, is he going to keep her on at Coningsby by herself? Or what?'

The afterthought sent a wave of panic sweeping through Hannah. 'Or what?' she repeated. What happened to pedigree Highland cattle if they couldn't be sold to another specialist breeder?

'Tell us!' Helen prompted.

But Eddie Huby refused to put it into words. As the tall, jerky figure of Terence Cooke reappeared at the end of Market Street, signalling another Land-rover and trailer through a narrow space, Hannah and Helen melted back towards the Curlew.

'I suppose he could send Skye to market again,' Hannah whispered, staring out through the window from the safety of the cafe.

'If her leg mends in time.' Helen pictured the lonely little calf shivering in one of the small metal pens at the cattle market.

They watched Eddie lead the first of the cows down the ramp and up into Grindleford's trailer. The ramp rocked under her weight, and she gave a shake of her matted fringe.

' . . . Or he could decide to keep Skye at Coningsby,' Hannah suggested.

'Git on!' Cooke shouted at the reluctant cow.

Helen shook her head. 'You heard what he said to Mrs Cooke. "Not a single beast to be kept!" '

'Does that include his hens?' Hannah said suddenly, remembering the pretty green Anconas pecking at grain on the floor of the barn, and proud Oscar strutting his stuff. 'Is a hen a beast?'

'Dad, is a hen a beast?' Helen asked David Moore, who had just come out from the kitchen with a tray of fresh scones.

'You've got me there.' He frowned, then laughed. 'No, I'd say a beast only covers four-legged stock, and a hen comes under the fowl bracket.' He put down the tray and came to see what they were looking at. 'Why?'

Hannah stared out at the second Kyloe being loaded into Grindleford's trailer. 'Nothing,' she said vaguely.

Helen decided to keep quiet about their visit to Mr Cooke's farm too. True, they were worried about Oscar, but right now they couldn't explain.

'Git on!' Fred Hunt waved his arms at his herd of Friesians to shoo them out of the milking parlour at High Hartwell into the next door cowshed.

Helen and Hannah sat on the farmyard gate watching in silence. Speckle sat to one side with Seth, Fred's alert and skinny farmyard dog.

'What are you two looking so happy about?' The old farmer treated them to a dose of sarcasm as he came out of the shed. It was Sunday morning. The autumn mists hung low over the fells and swirled into the valleys. 'You're sitting there looking like a couple of wet weekends,' he complained. 'Pretty much like the weather, as a matter of fact.'

'Leave them alone, Fred.' Hilda came by in her wellingtons and overcoat, carrying an empty bucket. 'They're upset.' She gave him a meaningful look then went on her way.

Hannah and Helen had poured out their troubles to Hilda over a cup of hot chocolate at her kitchen table. Their dad had received his bill from the garage, and was still waiting with dread for Terence Cooke to publicly blame him for the accident. The farmer's wife had been on their side, but told them she couldn't interfere.

'If you think I can make Fred change his mind about being a witness, you'll have to think again,' she'd told them. 'I've been married to him for over forty years and never once got him to shift his point of view!'

'Upset about what?' Fred asked them now. He wiped his hands down the front of his woollen jacket and came to lean on the gate. 'Didn't you find your witnesses, like I told you?'

Shoulders slumped, with downcast eyes, they told him what had happened.

'There's no need to try and get round me with a sob-story,' he warned. 'My mind's made up about not going to court.'

'We weren't trying to get round you,' Helen sighed. They'd shown up at High Hartwell because they'd been walking Speckle on the fell and Hilda had invited them in.

'No?' He cocked his head to one side and bent to pat Speckle. 'You weren't thinking of getting me to take on a couple of fancy Highland cattle alongside my good old Friesians, were you?'

Hannah shook her head. But she widened her eyes and glanced at Helen. The farmer had just sown the seed of an idea. 'You know Mr Cooke's selling his herd, then?'

Mr Hunt sniffed noisily. 'The whole of the Lake District knows, I shouldn't wonder. But most of the farmers round here have got more sense than to invest in Kyloes. Yes, they're hardy beasts and they don't cost a lot to feed, but they're slow to mature and they don't produce enough milk.' He shook his head. 'No, if you ask me, Terence Cooke will have to look further afield for his buyers.'

As Helen glanced back at Hannah and sighed, a cloud of steam gathered in the cold air. 'Eddie Huby says he won't find a buyer at all for Skye,' she said quietly.

'Ah. How is the little heifer?' The farmer took fresh interest in the calf he'd helped to save. 'I hear Eddie's worried about her.'

'Not eating. And her leg doesn't seem to be healing properly,' Hannah reported. She gazed longingly at Mr Hunt. *Just one little tiny Kyloe*! she thought. *Surely you have room*!

'Pity,' he murmured, softening for a moment. Then he briskly changed the subject. 'And now they've got something else to worry about over at Coningsby.'

'What?' Hannah and Helen jumped down from the gate and walked with him across the yard. Speckle trotted close behind.

'Haven't you heard?' Fred whistled Seth to come out with him into the field. 'It's that prize cockerel of Cooke's that's caused the problem this time.'

'Oscar?' they chorused.

'The fancy Faverolle. Gold head and neck, red and white feathers, black tail.'

'That's him!' Helen said.

'Missing,' Fred told them abruptly, setting off across the pasture with a rapid stride. 'Middle of last night. They got up this morning, and there was no sign of him.'

'Did he escape from the barn?' Hannah yelled after him.

'Escape?' The farmer paused and turned, while Seth streaked ahead. 'No, that's not what happened. From what I hear it's more likely that the precious thing's been stolen!'

Eight

'The word is that Mr Cooke is genuinely upset about Oscar,' Hilda Hunt told the twins when they ran to her inside the house to find out more. 'Eddie Huby says it looks like the final straw. His boss really loved that bird, poor man!'

'Poor man!' Hannah echoed. She connected Terence Cooke with words like 'angry' and 'frightening', not 'poor'.

Helen was already moving on; thinking fast and planning. 'Come on!' she hissed at Hannah, dragging her away from High Hartwell.

They said goodbye to Hilda and ran with Speckle across the fields.

'How come people feel sorry for Mr Cooke?' Hannah protested. 'How about "Poor Oscar"?'

'Forget that.' Helen wanted to share her plan. 'Listen, we're going to help Mr Cooke get Oscar back!'

Hannah nearly tripped over a heather bush with surprise. She leaned against a nearby wall to catch her breath. 'H-h-help Mr Cooke?'

'Yes. Here's why.' Helen had to be clear and quick. 'Reason number one: if Oscar has been stolen, he could be in danger.'

'OK.' Hannah nodded. She could sympathise with any creature in trouble.

'Number two: Mr Cooke loves Oscar. If we find the cockerel and take him back home, Mr Cooke will be grateful!'

'Ye-es?' This time Hannah couldn't be quite so sure.

'Third reason: Mr Cooke will want to know how he can thank us. We'll tell him two ways . . .'

'One: by letting Mrs Freeman come to treat Skye again.' Hannah followed Helen's line of thought more easily now.

'Yes. And that means Skye will get better quicker.' Helen stood face to face with her sister to make her see the sense of the plan.

'And she'll stand more chance of being bought by a good owner!'

'Exactly! And two: we'll say that Mr Cooke can show how grateful he is to us for getting Oscar back by letting Dad off the hook!' This was the masterstroke; the very best bit of Helen's plan. 'It's called killing two birds with one stone! Come on!'

She dragged Hannah on towards Home Farm, to cadge a lift from David Moore when he went in to Nesfield that afternoon to help their mum at the Curlew.

'Why is Hannah looking shell-shocked?' Mr Moore asked suspiciously, studying his daughter's dazed face. He'd already agreed to drive them into town. Now he was making them eat lunch before they set off. 'What are you up to, Helen?'

'We're going to find Oscar and get Mr Cooke to stop blaming you for the accident!' she announced, skipping all the bits in between.

'You are?' David Moore gave her a quizzical

glance. 'Just like that?' He recognised her reckless, wild look. Helen's hair had blown into tangles and her cheeks were flushed from running all the way from High Hartwell.

'But why are we going into town with Dad?' Hannah wanted to know. Oscar had disappeared from Coningsby Hall, which was nowhere near Nesfield.

Helen held up her fingers to begin another list. 'One: we can't pick up the trail at the Hall because Mr Cooke would get Eddie to throw us out. And two: . . .'

'I know, don't tell me!' Hannah had suddenly remembered something that the stockman had told them just before Mrs Cooke had unexpectedly turned up at Coningsby. 'You're telling me that we're going to look for Oscar in Nesfield because that's where Mr Cooke's wife is staying!'

'What's Judi Cooke got to do with it?' Their dad broke off from clearing away the dishes.

'It's obvious!' To Helen it was as clear as could be. Sometimes grown-ups could be so slow. 'Mr Cooke is mad with Mrs Cooke for leaving him. He sells all the Kyloes to get his own back. Now she's so mad with him, she'd do anything to upset him back. What does she do? She thinks of the thing that will hurt him the most . . .'

' . . . Goes back to the Hall in the dead of night and steals Oscar!' Hannah explained, suddenly seeing the light.

'And I used to think Nesfield was a tiny place!' Hannah slumped forward over an empty table by the window at the Curlew Cafe.

For hours they'd tramped the streets looking for any clue that would tell them where Mrs Cooke was living. They'd bumped into Sophie and Karl Thomas from Rose Terrace and asked them if they'd heard of anyone new moving in during the last week. They'd asked at the shops around the square, and in the smartly-painted guest-houses that lined every street in town.

'No luck?' Mary Moore asked. Business in the cafe was slowing down in late autumn, so she had time to sit down for a chat.

Helen shook her head. 'Not so far. And we've tried most of the places we can think of.'

'You would think a cockerel wouldn't be a hard

thing to find in a place like this.' Their mum considered the question of the missing bird. 'They're not exactly quiet creatures!'

'Maybe Mrs Cooke didn't bring him back into town,' Hannah sighed. 'Or maybe it wasn't her who stole him after all.'

'How much is a prize Flavourful worth?' David Moore put in. He too had his doubts. 'Would he be worth stealing?'

Helen tutted. 'Oscar is a *Faverolle*, not a *Flavourful*! And it's not for how much he's worth in money that he's been stolen. It's all because Mrs Cooke hates Mr Cooke.'

'You think so?' Her dad raised his eyebrows and began to clear some tables, humming as he worked.

'She must do!' Helen still saw it as black and white. 'Anyway, we're wasting time talking. If we want to track Oscar down before tea-time, we'd better get a move on.' Forcing her tired legs into action again, she stood up and scraped her chair along the floor. 'Where now?' she asked Hannah.

'Let's try the guest-houses down by the lake.' Like Helen, Hannah wasn't ready to give in. 'We'll start at this end and work our way along.'

Mary Moore smiled up at her. 'Trust you, Hannah. I always say you're the only one in our family with any sense of organisation.' She saw them to the door and waved them off. 'Be careful!'

Helen and Hannah waved back.

They headed straight for Lake Rydal, with its wooden jetty stretching out into the cold, clear water. Small rowing-boats were moored along the pebble beach, while half a dozen quiet swans glided further from the shore.

'Honeysuckle Cottage.' Hannah marched along the path that bordered the lake and turned in at the first gate. She remembered the neat flower borders, the trim creepers growing up the side of the house, and the stout figure of the landlady appearing through the frosted glass.

'Hello!' The woman recognised them too. 'Not still looking for Mr and Mrs Kirk, I hope?'

'No. But we'd like to know if a Mrs Cooke has booked in here, please.' Helen spoke politely, without much hope.

The landlady shook her head. 'I'm sorry.' She had the same kind smile, the same firm way of closing the door as before.

'Wait!' Hannah thought of another question. 'Have you heard anyone mention a cockerel called Oscar?'

The door stopped closing and the landlady peered round it with a puzzled look. 'A cockerel? What about it?'

'We're looking for him to take him back home,' Helen explained.

'Oh, yes *please*!' Now the door opened wide again. The landlady heaved a big sigh. 'I've never heard such a racket in all my life! Screeching and cackling like that at the top of his voice. He made enough noise to waken the dead!'

'When? Where?' For a mad moment, Hannah could have flung her arms around the landlady.

'This morning before dawn. It woke the whole row of houses, frightened the life out of me! It suddenly appeared in Mr Watson's garden shed. Came out of nowhere; no warning or anything like that. We thought it must have escaped from one of the farmers' Land-rovers when he was driving through town yesterday evening. There was a great fuss until my next-door-neighbour managed to track it down. Apparently the bird belongs to a lady who's renting a room on the ground floor.'

'Is he still in Mr Watson's shed?' Helen wanted to rush and see. But first she checked her facts.

'I think so. Why not go and ask? As far as I'm concerned, you can't take him back where he belongs soon enough!'

Her voice followed them down the path and into next door's garden. They ran and knocked at the door, waited impatiently on the top step for an answer.

'There's no one in!' Helen muttered. She darted along another path to peer down the side of the house. A long garden stretched towards the lake. There were tall hedges to either side, and a large wooden shed at the far end.

'That's where Oscar must be!' Hannah joined her and pointed.

'He's being pretty quiet,' Helen whispered. She pictured the proud, jaunty cockerel cooped up in the dark shed.

'So would you be, if you'd been kidnapped in the middle of the night!' She glanced up at the tall, gabled wall at the side of the house. 'I wonder where Mrs Cooke is?'

'Are you thinking what I'm thinking?'

Hannah nodded. 'If there's no one in, we could kidnap him right back!'

So they edged into the back garden, down a long, smooth lawn. A black cat crossed their path, creeping out of the hedge bottom and slinking smoothly past.

'Bring us good luck!' Helen breathed.

They drew near the shed, listening hard for a sign that Oscar was still there.

'The door's locked.' Hannah got there first and saw the padlock. She glanced back at the house, saw an open window glint, imagined a curtain moving.

'I can see through this window.' Helen stood on tiptoe to peer into the shed. She made out a lawn mower, garden forks and spades, an upturned wooden crate near to the door.

A beady black eye stared back at her from the top of the crate. Wings spread wide. A yellow beak opened and a scarlet comb rose on a golden head.

'Please don't!' Helen breathed.

Too late. Oscar saw Helen and crowed.

Hannah put both hands over her ears as the piercing cry tore through the air. Helen jumped back from the window. Then the back door of the house

opened and a slight, brown-haired figure came running.

'It's Mrs Cooke!' Helen cried, dragging Hannah round the back of the shed. They cowered in some bushes, looking in vain for a way through the thick, prickly hedge.

Oscar crowed on. He scrabbled and fluttered inside the shed, beating his wings against the wooden sides.

'I know you're there, so you may as well come out,' the landowner's wife said calmly from the end of the lawn.

Slowly disentangling themselves from the spikes and bare branches of the hedge, Hannah and Helen emerged. Helen brushed dead leaves from her jacket. Hannah stared miserably at a bleeding scratch on her hand.

Mrs Cooke frowned. 'It's quite obvious why you're here, so I won't ask.'

'Could we explain, please?' Hannah tried to speak above the row that Oscar was making.

'It's not how it looks,' Helen pleaded.

'You mean, you weren't about to steal *my* cockerel?' Mrs Cooke folded her arms and exaggerated the 'my'.

'But . . .' Hannah began.

' . . . We thought Oscar belonged to Mr Cooke!' Helen finished.

They both remembered the argument in the yard at Coningsby over who owned the cattle.

Mrs Cooke gave a hollow laugh. 'Terence may act as if he owns the whole world, but it's not necessarily true!' She half turned away to unlock the shed door. Then, to Helen and Hannah's surprise, she began to cry.

Hannah started forward. 'Please, Mrs Cooke . . .'

Mrs Cooke held up her hand, then wiped the tears from her cheeks. Her lip was still trembling, but she managed to speak at last. With a wobbly voice, almost drowned by the din from Oscar, she poured out her heart.

'The whole truth about my husband, if you must know . . .'

'Mrs Cooke, don't!' Helen backed away in embarrassment.

She went on regardless. ' . . . is that he cares more about his precious pedigree cows and hens than he does, ever did, or ever will, care about me!'

Nine

Hannah and Helen knew how to help animals in trouble. But when grown-ups cried they were at a loss.

'What do we do now?' Helen hissed. Her plan had backfired. It seemed they would never get Oscar back to Coningsby.

Hannah took a deep breath. She wanted to tell Mrs Cooke that it couldn't possibly be true; that Mr Cooke must care for her, or else why would he be so upset when she left? But the words stuck in her throat.

'Can't anyone stop that din?' A man's bald head

appeared over the hedge from the next garden in the row. 'I can't hear myself think for the racket that bird is making!'

The neighbour stamped off up his garden. But someone else called from further away. 'Whose cockerel is that? It's woken my baby from her afternoon nap!'

Then a car drew up in the street, a door slammed and the owner of the house appeared on the side path.

'Mr Watson?' Helen ran for help.

The man nodded. He was small and tubby, with a bushy beard and short grey hair. 'What's going on?' he demanded, casting a wary eye at Judi Cooke. 'Haven't you got rid of that bird like I asked?'

'She's upset,' Helen explained.

'I can see that. But I meant what I said; no pets on the premises. It's one rule that I never break.'

'No, that's not what she's upset about.' As Oscar let out an especially loud and long crow from inside the shed, Helen covered her ears. She ran alongside the landlord as he went to speak sternly to his new tenant.

'. . . But there's nowhere else for him to go!' Mrs Cooke sobbed.

When Helen took her hands away, the argument was already underway. She stood with Hannah, peering in through the shed's dusty window, trying to spot where Oscar had got to. He'd gone suddenly quiet and disappeared from sight.

'That's not my problem.' Mr Watson refused to budge. 'If I let you keep that bird in my shed, none of my neighbours will ever speak to me again.'

Hannah stood on tiptoe and pressed her face against the window. Where was Oscar? Why had he stopped crowing? 'Mrs Cooke . . .' she began.

'Just for a short while!' Judi Cooke pleaded again.

Mr Watson shook his head.

'Mrs Cooke, we can't see Oscar. He's vanished!' Helen cried.

'He can't have!' The distressed woman spun round and dug in her pocket for the key to the padlock. 'He must be in there somewhere!'

Hannah and Helen stood back. Maybe Oscar had found a secret way out; a loose floorboard, or a gap in one of the walls. They crept round the back of the shed to make sure, dropping on to all fours to search the bottom of the hedge and the space between the shed floor and the damp earth below.

'Nothing!' Helen muttered. She brushed twigs and leaves from her trousers and came round to the front again, just as Judi Cooke finally unlocked the door.

'Oscar?' She let the door hang wide as she peered inside.

For a moment there was silence. Then a rush of feathers, a squawk and a flash of red, black and gold. The sneaky cockerel made his great escape.

Out of the shed and up the lawn his feathered legs fled. He screeched and flapped, cackled at the

black cat who arched her back at him from the safety of an apple tree. He trampled over Mr Watson's flower beds, head stretched, wings spread wide, heading for freedom.

'It was a trick!' Hannah gasped. Oscar had gone quiet on purpose, waiting for the door to be opened.

'Quick!' Helen gathered her wits and set off after him. 'Stop him!' she called to the landlady at Honeysuckle Cottage, who had come to her front gate to see what the row was about.

The stout woman stepped out in front of Oscar. He swerved into the road and sprinted on.

Hannah and Mrs Cooke set off after Helen and Oscar. The cockerel crossed the road and rushed squawking on to the pebble beach at the water's edge.

Two swans snaked their long necks towards him and beat their mighty wings. Oscar fled in the opposite direction, dashing over the smooth grey pebbles towards the jetty.

'Stop that bird!' Hannah pleaded with a tourist who had been sitting by the lake quietly eating his sandwiches.

The man stood up with a start as the cockerel

charged towards him. 'Get off!' he yelped, grabbing his sandwich box from the ground and clutching it to his chest.

Oscar flashed by, his long black tail feathers ruffled by the breeze, his legs going like pistons along the beach.

People stopped their cars to watch the chase. Walkers in boots and anoraks looked on bemused.

'He's heading for the jetty!' Helen gasped. She saw her mum and dad come to the door of the cafe which overlooked the boats and wooden pier and yelled at them for help.

'If he runs along the jetty, we can trap him!' Hannah cried. She and Helen had left Mrs Cooke trailing behind. But they weren't quick enough to keep up with Oscar, who darted ahead, in and out of the surprised onlookers.

Oscar reached the line of moored boats. He flapped his wings and half-hopped, half-flew from one to the next.

'Woah!' someone cried, as the cockerel almost slipped and fell.

He recovered and scrambled back on to the shore.

'Dad, grab him for us!' Hannah saw David Moore

cross the road and run on to the beach. He was nearer to Oscar; only a few steps away, and the bird hadn't spotted him.

David crouched and crept up from behind. He and the twins formed a pincer movement to trap the runaway bird. Oscar hopped from the final boat on to the jetty, turned and saw them. They froze.

The cockerel's beady black eye flicked, his comb and wattles quivered as he thrust out his golden chest. 'Catch me if you can!' he seemed to crow. Lifting his feet high, strutting as he went, he stepped out along the wooden pier.

'Leave this to me!' David Moore whispered to Hannah and Helen. 'He's chosen a dead end. When he reaches the end of the jetty, there's nowhere for him to go!'

Oscar strutted on. Ahead of him was an expanse of water and sky. Mountains rose from the far shore, small boats sailed by.

Slowly, quietly, the twins' dad climbed up on to the jetty. He stretched out his arms, ready to pounce, then he tiptoed forward after the bird.

'This is it!' Helen whispered, as Oscar reached the end of the pier.

He ducked his head over the edge and saw the smooth, clear water. He flapped his wings and hopped on to a stout mooring-post, turned and waited.

David Moore crept closer.

'Catch him for me, please!' Judi Cooke had caught up at last. She saw the man crouched close to the perched bird and cried out in panic.

Oscar flapped, David Moore pounced. His outspread arms closed in on thin air as the jaunty cockerel took one hop too many.

Splash! Oscar landed in the lake.

'Ooh! . . . Oh!' Onlookers gasped.

Helen and Hannah ran along the jetty after Oscar.

Splash! David Moore jumped into the water to save the bird. He landed waist-deep and roared, 'It's freezing!'

Hannah reached the end of the jetty and dropped to her hands and knees. 'Quick, Dad, grab him before he sinks!'

Oscar flapped and squawked. His sodden feathers dragged him down.

David Moore plunged after him, arms flailing, until at last he drew near.

'He's going under!' Hannah cried.

Poor Oscar couldn't stay afloat much longer.

Their dad lunged again. This time he scooped the cockerel from the water. Oscar beat his bedraggled wings and protested loudly. But he was well and truly caught.

'Saved!' The crowd clapped and cheered.

Helen dragged Hannah to her feet and hugged her. Mrs Cooke fell sobbing into Mrs Moore's arms.

'Thank you, thank you!' Judi Cooke laughed and cried.

They were all back at the Curlew, warm and dry. David Moore had struggled out of his sodden jeans and jumper into fresh clothes. Oscar was wrapped in a towel on Mrs Cooke's lap.

'I'm so sorry. This is all my fault.' She shook her head and stroked the cockerel. 'If I hadn't taken Oscar away from his lovely big barn, none of this would ever have happened!'

' Never mind. He's safe now.' Mary Moore was handing out cups of tea. The cafe was closed and dusk was falling over the quiet lake.

'Does Oscar want something to drink?' Hannah asked anxiously. She was worried that his drenching hadn't done him any good. He sat huddled inside the towel, his comb drooping, his feathers still dull and damp.

'Water,' Mrs Cooke suggested.

So Hannah went for a bowl and set it down on the floor. She watched as Mrs Cooke tried to get the bird to drink by dipping his beak gently in the water. At first he wobbled on shaky legs, but soon he grew steady. His beak clicked against the side of the bowl as he began to drink.

'I only did it because I was so cross with Terence,' Judi Cooke murmured. 'I panicked when I heard he was selling all our lovely Highland cattle.' She sighed and wiped away the last of her tears. 'But I never gave a thought to poor Oscar when I did it, and when I shut him inside the horrid, dark shed, I didn't care that he was unhappy. All I could think of was getting my own back.'

'What will you do now?' Hannah asked. She squatted beside the cockerel as he drank.

Mrs Cooke stood up and shook David Moore's hand. She squared her shoulders, ready to face the consequences of what she'd done. 'I'm going to get in my car and drive him straight back home!'

Ten

Helen and Hannah sat with Oscar on the back seat of Mrs Cooke's car. They held him tight as the car climbed the hill and swung round the tight bends of Snakestone Pass. Down in the dark valleys, clusters of white lights showed the villages and towns.

'I'll talk to Terence and ask him to let Sally Freeman take another look at Skye,' Judi Cooke promised. She'd heard the full story of the accident from the twins.

'No one will want to buy her if her leg doesn't heal,' Hannah explained.

'And Eddie's really worried about her.' Helen saw the lights of Coningsby Hall ahead. As they came up the drive, she clutched Oscar more tightly and noticed that Hannah had all her fingers crossed once more.

Mrs Cooke pulled up quietly by the front of the house. 'I don't understand it,' she murmured, taking the cockerel from Helen. 'Skye was Terence's favourite calf.'

'Yet she was the first one he tried to sell,' Hannah pointed out.

'Probably because he knew she was my favourite too.' The worried frown on Mrs Cooke's face deepened as she told Helen and Hannah to wait by the car for a while. 'Give me five minutes to talk to Terence, then come round the side of the house into the yard,' she said, tucking Oscar under her arm and heading up the steps to the main door.

'Five minutes!' Helen sighed as the door closed behind her. It sounded like an age.

'She has to give Oscar back and say she's sorry.' Hannah pictured the scene somewhere inside the grand house. 'Then *he* has to say he's sorry too, and he's glad Oscar's back home. Then *she* has to tell him that it's thanks to Dad that Oscar didn't drown . . .' She paused to listen to voices in the yard.

'Someone's already out there.' Helen had heard them too. 'It sounds like Eddie.'

'He's talking to a woman.' Hannah frowned and fidgeted. Glancing up at the house, she could see the outlines of two people deep in conversation through the blinds in a downstairs room. The minutes were ticking by.

'Is it time to go and see?' Helen hopped from one foot to the other. Who was Eddie Huby talking to? Why were there footsteps going in and out of the barn?

Without realising they were doing it, Helen and Hannah left Mrs Cooke's car and crept around the side of the house.

'I'll have to re-set the bone,' the woman's voice was saying as they rounded the corner.

There was a Land-rover in the yard with Doveton Veterinary Service written on the side. Eddie Huby held the back door open as someone else leaned inside.

'Mrs Freeman!' Hannah and Helen said out loud.

Eddie glanced up and frowned. 'What are you two doing here?'

'We came with Mrs Cooke,' Hannah said.

'We'll explain later. But what are *you* doing?' Helen sped across to Sally Freeman.

'Taking another look at Skye,' the vet said, puzzled by the question. 'And not before time. One end of the broken bone has shifted out of position somehow. We need to start all over again.' Swiftly she swung her bag out of the Land-rover and hurried into the barn.

'How come?' Hannah whispered to the stockman. 'Did you persuade Mr Cooke to let her come?'

Eddie blushed. 'I did keep having a go at him,' he confessed. 'Laid it on thick, telling him the little heifer was in a bad way.'

'And he actually listened to you?' Helen walked eagerly beside him as he followed the vet.

'Let's say he had a change of heart,' Eddie said modestly. 'At about tea-time he came in and had another look at her. That was when he said he might have been a bit hasty.'

'At the same time as Oscar fell in the lake!' Hannah whispered. Mr Cooke wasn't the only one who'd been hasty and had a change of heart.

'So I sent for Mrs Freeman and she came as quick as she could.'

They walked after her down the rows of cattle stalls, to the pen at the far end, where Skye was kept.

'Hold her head,' Mrs Freeman told Eddie. She got to work straight away. 'And Hannah; you see those giant clippers there in my bag? Could you hand them to me, please?'

Hannah did as she was told, watching anxiously as the vet used the clippers to cut away the old plaster cast from Skye's hind leg.

'This time we'll use a longer, specially shaped splint, to cover more of the leg and hold the broken section more firmly in place,' she told them. She gave Helen pieces of the old cast and asked for more instruments.

'Why won't she eat?' Helen asked. Close to, she could see how dull Skye's eyes were. Her broad pink nose was dry, her head hanging low.

'Probably because she's been in too much pain. And there may be some infection in the broken limb. That would cause a fever and kill her appetite. Don't

worry, I'll give her more antibiotics to clear it up.'
Mrs Freeman gently shifted the calf so that she could
move in with the new splint.

They were concentrating so hard, quietly soothing
the calf as the vet worked, that no one heard the
warring owners walk into the barn.

' . . . Let's put it behind us,' Terence Cooke was
saying. 'Oscar's back safe and sound. That's all that
matters.'

Hannah glanced up and blinked. Did Mr
Cooke actually have his arm around Mrs Cooke's
shoulder?

'And you promise not to sell any more of the
cows?' Judi Cooke pleaded.

Her husband nodded. 'I'll cancel all the other
deals. I'll even phone Grindleford and try to get back
the four I sold to him if you like.'

Helen stared. The landowner was smiling and
hugging his wife.

'Bandage, please!' Sally Freeman held out her hand
and waited.

Hannah grabbed the bandage to strap the new
splint in place.

' . . . And while we're about it, you'll drop all the

nonsense about blaming David Moore for the silly accident,' Mrs Cooke went on.

Terence Cooke cleared his throat and frowned at Hannah and Helen. They glanced at Eddie Huby. Eddie blushed violently.

'After all, it's silly to bear a grudge. All that matters is that Skye is going to get better.'

The couple drew near to the patient's stall and watched the vet at work.

'She'll never be worth what she once was.' Mr Cooke shook his head.

Helen and Hannah sagged and sighed. He was never going to let their dad off the hook.

'Erm . . . Mr Cooke . . .' Eddie spoke up at last, stumbling over his words. 'About the traffic lights. I may have been coming down the hill a bit too fast . . .'

'Stop!' The landowner brushed the stockman's confession aside and hugged his wife. 'Judi's right. What good will blaming anyone do? No, from now on I plan to let bygones be bygones!'

Hannah dropped the scissors she was holding. They landed with a clatter on the stone floor.

'Can we tell our mum and dad?' Helen asked. She

knew her mouth was gaping open, but she was too amazed to shut it.

'No need. I'll ring them myself.' Mr Cooke turned, arm in arm with his wife, to go back to the house. But they stopped when another car drove up and the people in it, following the sound of voices, made their way over to the barn.

'Mr and Mrs Hunt!' Hannah was the first to recognise their neighbours from High Hartwell.

Fred Hunt was dressed in Sunday-best collar and tie. But he still wore his battered flat cap and wellington boots. He came towards them at a steady pace, his eye on the sick calf. 'I've come to make an offer for the weanling,' he grunted at Mr Cooke. 'How much do you want?'

Behind him, Hilda nodded and smiled at the twins.

'You want to *buy* her?' Terence Cooke stuttered.

'That's what I said, isn't it? I asked you plain enough; how much?'

The landowner looked at his wife. 'Skye isn't for sale,' he stammered.

'Don't mess me about, Cooke. Everyone knows you want to get rid of the whole herd. Of course, I'm not expecting to pay the full price for one that's broken its leg. But if you let me have her for a decent price, I'll take her off your hands.'

Hilda smiled broadly at the twins. 'Don't look at me!' she whispered.

'I didn't know you took an interest in Highland cattle.' Mr Cooke shuffled and coughed. 'I thought you stuck to your Friesians.'

'Normally I would say yes, I do.' Fred Hunt ran his expert eye over Skye. 'She's lost weight since the accident, but I reckon I can soon put that back on her. I'd like her as a sort of pet, see. Something to keep Mrs Hunt happy.'

His wife smiled contentedly without blinking.

'Well?' the old farmer urged.

The two men and Judi Cooke retreated to a corner to discuss the offer.

'Five minutes ago Skye didn't have a single person in the world who wanted her!' Helen whispered.

'Now she has *two* homes she could stay at!' Hannah went and put an arm around the calf's neck. Which would it be; High Hartwell or Coningsby Hall?

'Nearly finished!' Sally Freeman had worked through it all, wetting the special bandage so that

the plaster formed a hard shell.

'Will Mr Cooke sell her after all?' Helen asked Eddie Huby.

He pulled his mouth down at the corners. 'She's a favourite round here,' he reminded her.

Skye's pink nose nuzzled Hannah's palm. Then she thrust her head through the bars of the pen and gave a soft, mooing call.

'*Cocka-doodle-doo!*' Oscar had wandered into the farmyard and came strutting down the barn. His chest was out, his tail feathers fluttering. '*I'm-back! Look-at-me!*'

Everyone laughed.

' . . . What do you say?' Fred Hunt went on driving his bargain for Skye.

Terence Cooke turned to his wife. 'It's up to you.'

Still she hesitated, smiling at the calf from a distance as Skye balanced on her newly set leg. She went over to stand beside Hannah and Helen.

'I'll give you another five pounds for her on top of what I last said. But that's my final offer!' Fred growled.

'How would you feel about having Skye as your next-door-neighbour?' Judi Cooke asked the twins. 'You could visit her whenever you liked if she went to live at High Hartwell.'

They took deep breaths and nodded. Their dark eyes shone. *If only, if only* . . .

'It's a deal!' Terence Cooke shook hands with Fred Hunt.

'Done!' the old farmer agreed.

Oscar reached the end of the barn. He flapped his wings and hopped on to the top rung of Skye's stall. The calf gave him a gentle nudge.

'She'll do,' Sally Freeman said at last. She packed away her needles, scissors and bandages.

'She'll more than do!' Fred contradicted proudly. He came and patted Skye's shaggy head. 'By the time I've got her over to High Hartwell, fed her up and looked after her for a few weeks, you won't recognise her. You know what she'll be then, don't you?'

Hannah and Helen nodded. 'A champion!'

They gave the answer in a loud chorus that echoed under the high roof, out across the yard and down the slopes of Doveton Fell.

HOME FARM TWINS
Jenny Oldfield

66127 5	Speckle The Stray	£3.50	❑
66128 3	Sinbad The Runaway	£3.50	❑
66129 1	Solo The Homeless	£3.50	❑
66130 5	Susie The Orphan	£3.50	❑
66131 3	Spike The Tramp	£3.50	❑
66132 1	Snip and Snap The Truants	£3.50	❑
68990 0	Sunny The Hero	£3.50	❑
68991 9	Socks The Survivor	£3.50	❑
68992 7	Stevie The Rebel	£3.50	❑
68993 5	Samson The Giant	£3.50	❑
69983 3	Sultan The Patient	£3.50	❑
69984 1	Sorrel The Substitute	£3.50	❑

All Hodder Children's books are available at your local bookshop, or can be ordered direct from the publisher. Just tick the titles you would like and complete the details below. Prices and availability are subject to change without prior notice.

Please enclose a cheque or postal order made payable to *Bookpoint Ltd*, and send to: Hodder Children's Books, 39 Milton Park, Abingdon, OXON OX14 4TD, UK.
Email Address: orders@bookpoint.co.uk

If you would prefer to pay by credit card, our call centre team would be delighted to take your order by telephone. Our direct line *01235 400414* (lines open 9.00 am–6.00 pm Monday to Saturday, 24 hour message answering service). Alternatively you can send a fax on *01235 400454*.

TITLE		FIRST NAME		SURNAME	

ADDRESS	

DAYTIME TEL:		POST CODE	

If you would prefer to pay by credit card, please complete:
Please debit my Visa/Access/Diner's Card/American Express (delete as applicable) card no:

Signature .... Expiry Date: ....

If you would NOT like to receive further information on our products please tick the box. ❑

ANIMAL ALERT SERIES
Jenny Oldfield

All Hodder Children's books are available at your local bookshop, or can be ordered direct from the publisher. Just tick the titles you would like and complete the details below. Prices and availability are subject to change without prior notice.

Please enclose a cheque or postal order made payable to *Bookpoint Ltd*, and send to: Hodder Children's Books, 39 Milton Park, Abingdon, OXON OX14 4TD, UK.
Email Address: orders@bookpoint.co.uk

If you would prefer to pay by credit card, our call centre team would be delighted to take your order by telephone. Our direct line *01235 400414* (lines open 9.00 am–6.00 pm Monday to Saturday, 24 hour message answering service). Alternatively you can send a fax on *01235 400454*.

TITLE		FIRST NAME		SURNAME	
ADDRESS					
DAYTIME TEL:				POST CODE	

If you would prefer to pay by credit card, please complete:
Please debit my Visa/Access/Diner's Card/American Express (delete as applicable) card no:

Signature .... Expiry Date: ....

If you would NOT like to receive further information on our products please tick the box. ❏